More great books by
Jenny Oldfield!

Extra Time
ISBN 1-842993-40-2

Pet School

(September 2005)

ISBN 1-842993-34-8

Order them directly from our website at
www.barringtonstoke.co.uk

Contents

Chapter 1
The Trap

Danny Dolan couldn't believe his luck. He was going out with Ellie Conner, the best-looking girl in school.

"How did you do that?" his older brother, Frankie asked.

Danny shrugged his shoulders and went red. He knew what Frankie was saying. How come Ellie had chosen *him*? Plain old Danny

Dolan with the uncool haircut and holes in his socks.

And Ellie was gorgeous. She had long, shiny, black hair and big, brown eyes. Her skin was smooth like satin, creamy-like ... Danny gave up. All he knew was that he was in love with Ellie Conner.

****

"Danny, watch what you're doing!" Joey Watkins yelled. They'd both stayed on after school for football training. Danny played centre for the school team. Joey was a fellow striker. Between them they'd scored twelve goals for their team that season.

"I said, wake up!" Joey yelled at Danny again.

The ball shot past Danny, out of play. He'd been dreaming of Ellie's silky, black hair instead of watching the ball.

Now Joey shoved past him to fetch it. "Jeez, Danny!" he muttered.

"Liven up, Dolan!" Mr Wood shouted at Danny from the centre line. "I'm teaching you the off-side trap. The tactic you use to get a goal disallowed. It's complicated, so you need to have your brain in gear!"

"Danny doesn't have a brain!" Joey sneered, arms raised over his head for a throw-in. "He used to have one, but it turned to mush when he started going out with Ellie Conner!"

"Ha ha! Very funny!" The cold rain got to Danny and he started to shiver. So he sprinted up the pitch to get warm and be ready to receive Joey's throw-in.

There was no-one between him and the goalmouth. Here was a chance to boot one into the back of the net. He collected the ball and dribbled it.

"Off-side!" Mr Wood blew the whistle to pull him up short. "Danny Dolan, look around you. Haven't you listened to a word I said about the off-side trap?"

Chapter 2
Football Crazy

"I want you all to log on now," Miss Robbins said.

Ellie sat beside her friend, Annie Lomax, in the I.T. room. They'd stayed on after school for extra help. A row of computers hummed and clicked. Screens flashed, arrows pointed.

Danny was out there playing football in the rain. Ellie could see him through the window in the distance. That loudmouth Joey Watkins was shoving him around. Danny looked small and cold.

"Scroll down," Miss Robbins told them.

"Poor Danny!" Ellie whispered to Annie.

"Poor Danny nothing!" Annie hissed back. "He loves getting frozen. It's his choice to kick a soggy ball in the rain. Football crazy is what he is!"

Annie knew she was right and Ellie knew it. Football was Danny's life. He ate, slept and dreamed football. Sometimes she thought he liked the game better than he liked her.

"Click the mouse!" Miss Robbins instructed.

Ellie's thoughts were miles away. What if Danny did love football better? True, he said he really liked her. They'd been to the disco, they'd watched videos at her house, she'd met his brother, Frankie and his dog, Fred. But ...

"Ellie, click the mouse!" Miss Robbins said again, more loudly.

She clicked.

Then she stared out of the window again at the boys playing footie in the rain. She felt a small flutter under her ribs, her heart pounded and her mouth went dry. She'd been going out with Danny Dolan for three short weeks.

But he'd been a football fan all his life.

Chapter 3
Ellie, Ellie, Ellie!

Danny sat on the bus on his way home. The bus swayed and splashed through the rain. It stopped at lights, crawled through the rush hour traffic and let people on and off with a swish of the automatic doors.

The three weeks he'd been going out with Ellie had been the best of his life so far.

Pictures flickered through his mind. Ellie dancing at the disco under flashing lights. Ellie and he walking hand in hand through the park. Ellie sitting on his sofa watching a video with Fred. Fred's furry head resting on her lap.

What was it about Ellie? Her hand was small and soft when he held it. She smiled a lot and let her hair fall forwards over her face. When he was with her he felt he was in heaven. The bus went past his stop and Danny didn't even notice.

Yeah, he just couldn't believe his luck.

****

Annie and Ellie walked home together after I.T. Ellie had confessed to Annie that she thought that maybe Danny liked football better than her.

"You must be joking," said Annie.

"But what if it's true?" Ellie insisted.

Annie had stopped her in a shop doorway. "Listen, Ellie, you needn't worry. Even if Danny did lose interest, you could still go out with any boy in the school!"

But that wasn't what Ellie wanted. She wanted skinny, shy, funny Danny with his scruffy dog. Danny with his pale grey eyes that looked right into hers.

So she rang him later that evening. "Hi, Danny."

"Hi, Ellie."

"Have you dried off yet?"

"After training? Yeah, I've dried off."

"Good ..."

"United played in a league match tonight. We won two-nil." Danny was excited.

"Good …"

"Jones scored both goals. One was a penalty."

"Great. Listen, Danny. Do you fancy coming ice-skating this Saturday?" Ellie had worked this out carefully. She knew that United were playing a big cup match that day. Ticket holders only. And Danny didn't have a ticket. So he should be free. But she didn't want to sound too keen. "I'm planning to go to Skating World with Annie and the others. Do you want to come?"

"Who'll be there?"

"Annie."

"Yeah, you said. And who else?"

14

"Callum, Ruth, Sam and Zoe. Don't worry, you're not the only boy." She tried to keep it light, but she was dying for Danny to put her out of her misery and say yes.

"Yeah, OK." He played it cool. "Might as well." Ice-skating wasn't his thing. Anyway, he'd rather be by himself with Ellie.

"OK, see you." Quickly she put down the phone. That didn't go too well, she thought. But at least he'd said yes.

Chapter 4
The Big One

Danny flung down the phone and went back to his seat on the sofa. "Move it, Fred!" Danny said crossly.

The dog sighed and shuffled further along the sofa to make room for Danny.

Danny picked up the remote control to see what was on. A game show. An old movie. The news. Click, click, click. A nature film about parrots.

Danny shook his head. How come he'd made a mess of the ice-skating thing? He'd made Ellie feel that he didn't really want to go. Great. That was smart ... not!

Frankie stuck his head around the door. "Hey, you, I'm going down the gym. How come you're watching a programme about parrots?"

"I'm not." Click. The screen went blank. Fred snored from his corner of the sofa.

"Listen, if Carli rings, tell her I'll call her tomorrow."

"Uh," Danny grunted. Carli and Frankie had been going out for months. They'd learned how to do their own thing. It didn't worry them.

The front door banged as Frankie went out. Danny waited ten seconds and then turned the parrot programme back on.

There was one bird, some kind of blue macaw thing that lived in the jungle in South America. It was the only one left of its kind in the whole world. Lonely, or what? Danny thought.

Then the phone rang again and he leapt up. He groped on the floor to find it, picked it up and spoke.

"Hey, Danny!" Joey Watkins said.

"What d'you want?" he snapped. He'd hoped it was Ellie ringing for another chat.

"Oh, very nice!" Joey joked. "I give you a call and nearly get my head bitten off."

"Sorry. What d'you want?"

"You're gonna be so grateful after I tell you what I'm holding in my hand right this minute!" Joey said. He enjoyed teasing Danny. "I mean, this is pure gold. People are killing to get these, believe me!"

"C'mon, tell me," Danny said. He felt the hair at the back of his neck prickle. "What's it about?"

"The match on Saturday!" Joey announced. "What else?"

The semi-final. The big one. "What about the match?"

"I've got tickets. Two of them!"

"You've got tickets for the cup match?" Danny gasped. They had been sold out for ages. No-one could buy them unless they knew the right person. "Are you winding me up?"

"No, I'm serious. I'm holding two tickets right here in my hand. Let me read it out to you. *United versus City.*" Joey came clean. "One of them's for you. Do you want it or not?"

Chapter 5
Idiot

Danny would kill to see the semi-final. He would lie, cheat and push his way through a heap of dead bodies. Well, almost. This was the chance of a lifetime.

But try explaining this to someone who didn't like football. Someone who happened to be your girlfriend. And whose dark brown eyes were flashing angrily at you outside the school gate.

"You promised to come ice-skating!"
Ellie told him. "And now you're telling me
you're going to a football match instead!"

It had been a hard choice. Danny had
tossed and turned in bed all night.

"Go to the match!" a voice inside his
head had whispered. "What harm can it do?"

"You'll make Ellie mad if you do!"
another voice warned.

"So?" Voice Number One took charge.
"She'll get over it. And you can't miss the
semi-final. Not when Joey went to all that
trouble to get you a ticket."

"Ellie won't like it!" Voice Number Two
warned, but not so loud this time.

"Just tell her it's important." Voice
Number One wouldn't leave him alone.
"She'll understand."

So he'd waited all day until the end of school. He kept saying to himself over and over, 'Ellie, I hope you don't mind, but I've got a ticket for *the* match. I won't be coming to Skating World after all'.

And he'd said it to her face at the school gate after the bell had gone.

"It's not just any old match," he tried to explain. "It's the big one. The semi-final."

Ellie stared at him. She didn't say anything.

"I can't miss it. Not now I've been offered a ticket."

Still nothing from Ellie. Only, the look she gave him made him feel like a rat. Her eyes had tears in them.

"I'll come skating after the match!" Danny tried to make it better.

Ellie turned away. "Don't bother!" she snapped. "Forget about it. You just go along to your stupid match and have a really great time!"

****

"Danny Dolan's an idiot," Annie told Ellie later that night. They were slipping and sliding along an icy pavement, heading for the youth club.

Annie was dressed to kill in high shoes and tight, black trousers. She wore glitter eye shadow and had sprayed streaks of pink into her fair hair. Ellie's long, dark hair hung loose around her shoulders. She didn't need glitter to make her eyes shine.

"I knew it would happen sooner or later," Ellie sighed. "When it comes to a standoff between me and football, I don't stand a chance!"

24

"Like I said, Danny's an idiot." Annie spotted some kids hanging around in the doorway. There was Sam Miller, Callum Cameron and Joey Watkins. She nudged Ellie in the ribs and giggled. "Never mind, plenty more fish in the sea to choose from!"

Chapter 6
Danny and Fred

Inside the youth club, Annie and Ellie sat drinking Coke. They watched Callum and Joey play snooker. Across the room Danny sat all alone.

"What do you think of Callum?" Annie whispered.

Ellie raised one eyebrow. "Please! I'm not that desperate!"

"OK, I agree. But how about Joey?"

Joey, the star striker of the school soccer team, leaned forward over the green table. He lined up a blue ball then smacked it into the pocket.

"Not bad," Ellie admitted.

Joey was six feet tall and fit. He took care of the way he looked and wore stuff that let you see his big chest and broad shoulders.

"He's cool!" Annie sighed. She'd spent six months working on Joey Watkins to get him to ask her out before she gave up.

Smack! Joey rattled another ball into a pocket. He chalked the end of his cue and strutted right in front of them.

"Yeah," said Ellie, "but there's a problem. He's in love with himself." Ellie drank her

Coke and tried not to notice Danny sitting in the corner with no-one to talk to.

****

Joey won the snooker game. Callum wandered over to the girls. "What happened with you and Danny?" he asked Ellie.

"Nothing. Why?" Callum was the third person to ask. He pointed to Danny's empty chair. "Danny just left without you."

"So?" Ellie said. She wanted to run and hide. She wanted to run after Danny and say sorry. She wanted a big hole to swallow her up.

"They had a row," Annie explained.

"We didn't!"

"They did. Danny wants to go to a

stupid footie match tomorrow instead of coming ice-skating with us." Annie didn't care who knew. In fact, she made sure that Joey and Sam could hear what she said. After all, there was no point Ellie moping after Danny now.

The boys came crowding round.

"We'll come skating if you ask us!" Callum cried, going down on his knees.

"You and Sam are already coming, nutcase!" Annie reminded him with an elbow shove. Then she turned to Joey and fluttered her sparkly eyelids. "How about you? Do you fancy coming ice-skating tomorrow afternoon instead of Danny?"

Joey was staring hard at Ellie. He glanced at the door Danny had just left by. Then he turned back to the snooker table and casually potted a stray ball. "Sure. Why not," he said. "As it happens, I don't have anything else planned."

****

Danny was back early from the youth club. He was on the old sofa. Danny and hairy Fred. Danny and the TV. He lay with his feet up, flicking the remote control.

He action-replayed what had happened with Ellie. She had been there but she hadn't even spoken to him. When she saw him, she turned away with a swish of that lovely, long hair. Then she'd started talking to Joey and Callum.

So here he was resting his feet on the dog. He felt like the lonely, blue parrot from the TV programme. *Squawk squawk*, no-one to talk to.

Except Fred.

"What would you have done, Fred," he asked, "if Joey had offered you a ticket for the semi-final? You'd have snapped his hand off to get that ticket, wouldn't you?"

The dog sighed and opened one eye. He wagged his stumpy tail. "Yeah, see. You would." Danny sat through an American sitcom without laughing once.

Then Frankie came in and had a word with Danny. "Why the long face?" he asked. "I thought you had a ticket for the match tomorrow. You should be over the moon."

Chapter 7
Dead Grannies?

There was a big crowd outside Gate E when Danny arrived at the football ground. This was where he'd arranged to meet Joey, half an hour before the start of the match.

Danny stood in the rain with his collar turned up. He wore his team scarf draped around his neck and stood with his hands in his jacket pockets.

He watched the fans go into the ground. There was a buzz as they got ready for the big one.

"I reckon we'll win two-nil," a United kid said as he went through the turnstile.

"Yeah, but City will play the off-side trap," his friend reminded him. "We'll have to watch that. Make sure they don't catch us out."

Two-nil would be good, Danny thought. We'd be through to the final for the second time in four years.

So where was Joey? What was keeping him? Luckily Joey had handed over Danny's ticket the day before. It was safe in his back pocket, so he could take his seat whether Joey showed up or not.

"Hey, Danny!" Frankie called from across the street. He jumped over a couple of puddles, dodged the cars and arrived at the gate. He waved a ticket in front of Danny's face. "Look what I've got!"

"How come?" Danny grinned at his brother, glad for him. Frankie had been a United fan even longer than he had.

"Magic!" Frankie kidded.

"No. How come really?" Danny was still looking out for Joey among the crowd.

"You can stop wondering what's keeping Joey," Frankie told him, pulling him towards the turnstile. "This is his ticket I'm holding in my hot little hand!"

"So how come?" Danny ran to keep up with Frankie, past the hot-dog stalls and the coffee machines. There was ten minutes to go before the start of the match so they had to hurry.

"It was like this," Frankie explained. He took the steps into the stand two at a time. "I was at home. I had my bike in bits all over the kitchen floor, cleaning it up. The radio was on and I was listening to the pre-match talk."

"Yeah, yeah." Danny wished Frankie would skip the boring bits. "And?"

"And suddenly Joey turns up out of the blue. He's in this big rush, asking me if I want to buy his ticket because something important has turned up and he can't go to the match after all."

"Jeez." Danny imagined how sick Joey must have felt. "That stinks."

"Yeah. So I grab the ticket before he changes his mind. And here I am." Frankie led the way along the row to their seats. He sat down and viewed the smooth, green pitch below. What was so important that Joey couldn't make the match? Danny wondered, sitting down beside him. It must be major, like his granny dying or something.

Anyway, the teams were jogging up the tunnel now.

The crowd was starting to roar. So Danny forgot Joey. He forgot Ellie and the row they'd had. And he focused on the game.

Chapter 8
Off-Side!

"Nil-nil," Frankie muttered at half-time. He shook his head in disgust.

"Yeah, we should be one-nil up," Danny said.

The ball had landed square in the back of the City net. United were already jumping around and hugging before the linesman put up his flag. "Goal disallowed!"

"No way was Nick Jones off-side!" Frankie and Danny agreed.

"But that's what City do. They keep their men back and play the off-side trap," Frankie shrugged. "It's a mean trick and it could backfire on them if they play it once too often."

Nil-nil at half-time. The game was on a knife edge. "We're the better team," Danny insisted. "We've got Jones and Brown up front and Hunter in defence."

By now the players had left the pitch for the team talk in the locker rooms. The crowd buzzed with hot debate over United's disallowed goal.

"You wait, we'll score two in the second half," Danny told Frankie. "Bet you're glad Joey couldn't make it?"

"Yeah, he doesn't know what he's missing," Frankie agreed. "And guess what? You won't believe this. He gave up his ticket on account of some girl!"

Danny looked sideways at his brother. "Come again?"

"Some girl!" Frankie repeated.

Not a dead granny or a major crisis. "What girl?"

Frankie shrugged. "Search me. Joey didn't give a name."

Danny sat up in his seat. He suddenly felt tense. In his mind he had a picture of Joey Watkins showing off his muscles. Joey at the youth club playing snooker in front of Ellie and Annie Lomax. Joey showing off for the girls.

"Relax, Danny," Frankie said. "It's Joey's problem if he gave up a semi-final ticket just to go poxy ice-skating!"

Talk about off-side! Talk about dirty, low-down tactics! Danny felt himself go hot and then cold.

Would Joey get Danny out of the way on purpose, then step in and make a move on Ellie?

Would even Joey stoop so low?

Yeah, he would.

Joey was six feet of muscle with the biggest head in the world. He was drop dead gorgeous and he knew it. And when Danny had turned up at the school disco with Ellie three weeks earlier, Joey had looked like an idiot.

Joey had already invited Ellie and she'd

refused. Then she'd shown up with Danny. The way Joey saw it, that was major insult time. And now was his big chance to pay Danny back, even if it did mean missing the match.

"... Danny, did you hear what I said?" Frankie nudged him. "I asked you if you wanted a Coke?"

He nodded and watched his brother work his way along the row. Then he glanced at the clock.

Right now, right this minute, Ellie was meeting up with Annie, Sam, Ruth, Callum, Zoe ... and Joey! No doubt about it. That was exactly what Joey had planned.

Danny stood up from his seat, felt dizzy, sat down again. The bloke two seats along gave him a funny look.

Danny pictured Ellie walking into

Skating World and putting on her ice
skates. Joey would wait for her and lead her
onto the ice. He would be the best skater in
the whole place. He would sweep Ellie off
her feet ...

Danny gulped hard and jumped up a
second time. He stumbled over people's feet
as he pushed his way past. Then he bumped
into Frankie who was carrying a can of
Coke.

"What's up? Are we sinking?" Frankie
joked. "Is this the *Titanic*? Did we hit an
iceberg? Abandon ship!"

"Get out of the way, Frankie!" Danny
gasped.

Frankie's jaw dropped open. "But you'll
miss the second half!"

"I know!" This was more important than
grannies dying. "I gotta go!"

Chapter 9
Ouch!

It took Danny two bus rides and a half mile walk to reach Skating World.

Danny saw the latest score in a TV shop window. United nil, City one after fifteen minutes' play in the second half. Hunter had given away a penalty. United's road to the final was looking grim.

It was getting colder and the wet pavement had frozen. Danny slipped and slid up the steep hill towards Skating World.

The woman behind the desk had the match playing on the radio. He asked her the latest score.

"One all," she told him. "Brown equalised in the sixty-second minute."

"Yes!" Danny punched the air and hurried on. "Hey, here's your token for hiring skates!" the woman called after him.

He ignored her and pushed his way through gangs of small kids, looking for Ellie.

Annie saw him before he spotted Ellie. "Hey, Danny, why aren't you at the match?" she cried at the top of her voice.

"Where's Ellie?" he asked. Was it too late? Was Joey Watkins already whizzing her around the rink? Danny looked desperately at the gliding, twirling figures.

Annie's eyes lit up when she worked out what was going on. Danny against Joey, fighting over Ellie. "Romantic, or what!" she sighed to Zoe and Ruth as Danny rushed away.

"Yeah, like *Romeo and Juliet!*" Zoe whispered.

"Like that girl in *Titanic!*" Ruth sighed.

Annie shook her head and stared. "He gave up the match for Ellie!"

****

Danny had reached the edge of the ice. He tried hard to pick out Joey's tall, fair figure and Ellie's black hair. A kid with a

blonde ponytail and a short skirt did a twirl nearby. Two boys sped past.

Then Danny heard Joey's loud voice. "Anybody can ice-skate," he was saying. He'd sat down to put on his skates, and now he stood up.

It turned out that he and Ellie had been getting ready only a few feet from where Danny stood.

Then Danny heard Ellie's anxious voice. "But you never tried it before!" Ellie was busy warning Joey and helping him onto the ice. She didn't spot Danny.

Joey refused to listen. "So what? It's like rollerblading. Anybody can do it."

Wobble wobble. Super athlete Joey Watkins took his first step on ice skates.

"It's not like rollerblading. It's different!" pleaded Ellie. She looked up and saw Danny standing there. His face was pale and serious, and he should have been at the match. So what was he doing over there?

"Watch me!" Joey boasted. He struck out towards the centre of the rink.

But Ellie was watching Danny.

He said nothing. He just stared back at her.

Joey set off in a straight line across the ice. He took another gliding step, right across the path of the little girl with the ponytail. She swerved to miss him. He flung out his arms and tried to slow down.

"Watch out!" the two speed skaters yelled.

Joey's arms waved like windmill blades. "How do I stop?" he shouted. He was out of control, heading for the barrier at the far side of the rink.

"Look at Joey!" Ruth called to Zoe and Annie. "Watch this." They held their hands in front of their eyes and cringed. "Ouch!"

Crash! Joey hit the barrier and fell down flat. A bunch of eight-year-olds skated around him or jumped over him as he lay there groaning.

Danny saw it out of the corner of his eye. He grinned. Ellie grinned back.

When Ellie smiled a light went on behind her eyes and lit up her whole face. "The trouble with Joey is, he never listens," she said.

Chapter 10
Highlights

That evening they played the highlights on TV.

Fred watched the goals, curled up on the sofa between Ellie and Danny. He was in doggy heaven.

"That was never a penalty!" Danny said when he saw the City striker brought down by Hunter in the goalmouth.

Ellie held Danny's hand and tried hard to understand the rules.

Then, when Jones scored the winner in the seventy-ninth minute, Danny leapt up from the sofa.

"Two-one, two-one!" he yelled, arms raised above his head, dancing around the room like an idiot. "*We're on our way to Wembley, we shall not be moved!* he sang.

"Explain this off-side thing again," Ellie said after Danny had calmed down.

Danny shoved Fred off the sofa and sat down beside her. "OK. City defenders tried to catch Jones in the off-side trap. They hung back when Brown passed the ball, expecting the linesman to raise his flag to give Jones off-side. But the referee said play on. Which meant there was only the goalie to beat. We scored the winner with eleven minutes to go. Get it?"

As Ellie shook her head, her hair swung across her cheek, black as a blackbird's wing, shiny and smooth as silk.

"Two-one to us. That's all that counts," Danny sighed. He slid his arm along the back of the sofa.

Ellie nestled against his shoulder. "You gave up the match for me!" she whispered. Now she knew how much she meant to him.

"Yeah, well ..."

The United fans sang the tune, "*We're on our way to Wembley,*" in the background. Danny's spirits soared like a bird.

Hair like a blackbird's wing ...

Pushing Fred's wet nose out of the way, Danny leaned sideways and kissed Ellie's soft, warm cheek.

Barrington Stoke would like to thank all its readers for commenting on the manuscript before publication and in particular:

Martin Chrimes
Mark Deed
Robert Ferguson
Lucy Godding
Ailsa Mackie
Brendan Macrae
Jocelyn Scott
Helen Spence

Become a Consultant!

Would you like to give us feedback on our titles before they are published? Contact us at the email address below – we'd love to hear from you!

Email: info@barringtonstoke.co.uk
Website: www.barringtonstoke.co.uk

If you loved this book, why don't you read ...

Extra Time

by Jenny Oldfield

ISBN 1842993-40-2

Have you ever fancied someone and thought you had no chance? Danny really likes Ellie but decides he's more likely to play in the FA Cup Final than to get a date with her. Ellie likes Danny too but thinks he's only interested in football. Will they ever get together?

You can order *Extra Time* directly from our website at **www.barringtonstoke.co.uk**

If you loved this book, why
don't you read ...

Nicked!

by David Belbin

ISBN 1-842991-90-6

Are you brave enough to catch a thief? Nick
means to find out who's stealing video
equipment from his school. But his efforts
backfire when the police suspect he is the
culprit. How can Nick convince them he is
not the criminal?

You can order *Nicked!* directly from our website at
www.barringtonstoke.co.uk

If you loved this book, why don't you read ...

Dream On

by Bali Rai

ISBN 1-842991-95-7

"If you dream, it must be for real ..."

Baljit's mates knew what was what. If you were good at football, really good, you could go places. But all his old man ever talked about was duty to the family and paying bills. Baljit couldn't just go on working in his old man's chippie. He wanted out!

You can order *Dream On* directly from our website at
www.barringtonstoke.co.uk

If you loved this book, why
don't you read ...

Second Chance

by Alison Prince

ISBN 1-842991-94-9

Ross's noisy family has been thrown out
again. This time there's nowhere to go –
except the old café on the beach. But odd
things have happened there. Who is the boy
watching Ross? Watching, and waiting?

You can order *Second Chance* directly from our website
at **www.barringtonstoke.co.uk**